. . . *Roads*

. . . Roads

By
Seabury Quinn

With illustrations
by Virgil Finlay

1948
Arkham House, Sauk City, Wisconsin

Copyright 1948, Renewed 1976, by Seabury Quinn, Jr.
Arkham House is a Trademark of Arkham House Publishers, Inc. Used With Permission

This reproduction of the original first edition is published by
Red Jacket Press, 3099 Maqua Place, Mohegan Lake, New York 10547
www.redjacketpress.com

ISBN 978-1-7062364-1-2

All Rights Reserved. No part of this book may be reproduced in any form without the
written permission of the licensor of the original work or the publisher.

Roads is also available in hardcover as a limited edition "facsimile" reprint volume, a
complete and detailed reproduction of the original first edition (published by Arkham
House in 1948), packaged in a deluxe gift box that includes a booklet with biographical
information about author Seabury Quinn and illustrator Virgil Finlay. The dust jacket and
gift box both feature the beautiful metallic gold ink of the original 1948 edition. Order
your copy at www.amazon.com/dp/097488958X

It's a long way round the year, my dears,
  A long way round the year.
I met the frost and flame, my dears,
  I found the smile and tear.
The wind blew high on the pine-topp'd hill,
  And cut me keen on the moor;
The heart of the stream was frozen still
  As I tapped at the miller's door.

I tossed them holly in hall and cot,
  And bade them right good cheer,
But stayed me not in any spot
  For I traveled round the year,
To bring the Christmas joy, my dears,
  To your eyes so bonnie and true,
And a mistletoe bough for you, my dears,
  A mistletoe bough for you.

                    —Virginia Woodward Cloud*

* By permission of Appleton-Century-Crofts, Inc.

. . . *Roads*

I. The Road to Bethlehem

P_{ILES} of blazing thornbush crackled in the base-court of the sari, camels grunted discontentedly in their kneeling places, horses munched dry grass. Around the empty cook-pots men licked grease and crumbs of millet from their fingers and brushed them from their beards, then drew their sheepskin cloaks about them and lay down upon the kidney stones to sleep: all but the three who huddled round a charcoal brazier in a corner by the horse lines—they were talking treason.

"*Wah*, these be evil days for Jacob's children, they are as the tribes in Egypt were, only they have neither Moses nor a Joshua! The tax of a denarius on every household, and each one forced to journey to his birthplace. . . . Now they slay our children in their swaddling-bands. . . . This Romans' puppet that sits on the throne, this unbelieving Greek!"

"But Judas will avenge our wrongs; men say that he is that Messiah we have waited for so long. He will rouse his men of valor out of Galilee and sweep the Roman tyrant in the sea—"

"*Sh-s-s-sh*, hold thy babble, Joachim; that one yonder is belike a spy!"

With one accord the men turned toward the figure hunched in sleep before a dying fire of thornbush. Flaxen-haired, fair-skinned, he drooped above the whit-

[6]

ening embers, his cloak of ruddy woolen stuff draped loosely round his shoulders, the sinking fire-glow picking out soft highlights on the iron cap that crowned his flowing, braided hair—a man of mighty stature, one of the gladiators kept by Herod in his school for athletes that was constantly replenished from the German provinces or the Slavic tribes beyond the Danube.

"What does the godless dog so far from Herod's kennels?"

"The Lord of Zion knows, but if he go back to the Holy City and tell the tale of what he has heard here, three crosses will crown Golgotha before another sun has set," Joachim interrupted softly, and dropping to his knees unloosed the dagger strapped to his wrist as he wormed his way across the courtyard flints. In all the country round about Jerusalem there was no hand more skillful with the knife than that of Joachim, the cut-purse.

[7]

Softly as the cat that stalks a mouse he crept across the stones, paused and bore his weight on one hand while he drew the other back . . . a single quick thrust underneath the shoulder-blade, slanting downward to the heart, then the gurgling, blood-gagged cry, the helpless thrashing of the limbs, the fight for breath, and—perhaps the sleeping gladiator had a wallet stuffed with gold, or even copper. They were well paid, these fighting mastiffs from Herod's kennels. The firelight glinted on the plunging knife, and on the golden bracelet clasped about the Northman's arm.

"Ho! little brother of a rat, would you bite a sleeping man?" the giant's bell-like voice boomed, "And one who never did thee any harm? For shame!" White lines sprang into prominence against the sun-gilt skin, his mighty muscles tightened, and a yelp of pain came from Joachim as the knife dropped from his unnerved

[8]

fingers and a crackling like the breaking of a willow twig told where his wrist bones snapped beneath the Northling's grip.

"Have mercy, mighty one," Joachim begged. "I thought—"

"Aye, that thou didst, thou niddering craven!" came the answer. "Thou thought me sleeping, and like the thief thou art were minded to have my purse and life at once. Now get thee gone from out my sight, thou and those hangdog friends of thine, before I crush that puny neck between my fingers."

He spread his hands, great well-shaped, white-skinned hands trained in the wrestler's art and in the wielding of the sword, and the strong white fingers twitched as though already they felt yielding flesh and snapping bone between them. With a frightened skirking, as though they were in truth the rats the Northman named them, the three con-

spirators slunk out, Joachim the cut-
purse nursing his broken right wrist in
the crook of his left arm, his two companions close beside him as they sought
to gain the exit of the courtyard before
the giant Norseman reconsidered and
repented of his mercy.

The blond-haired stranger watched
them go, then swung his cloak back
from his shoulders. Beneath the cape he
wore from neck to knee a tunic of fine
woolen stuff dyed brilliant red and
edged about the bottom with embroi-
dery of gold. A corselet of tanned bull-
hide set with iron studs was buckled
round his torso; his feet were shod with
buskins of soft leather laced about his
legs with rawhide thongs; from the girdle at his waist on one side hung a
double-bladed axe, on the other a soft
leather pouch that clinked with a metallic sound each time he moved. Between
his shoulders swung a long two-handed

sword with a wide well-tempered blade, pointed and double-edged. He was brawny and wide-shouldered, his hair was braided in two long fair plaits that fell on either side of his face beneath his iron skullcap. Like his hair his beard was golden as the ripening wheat, and hung well down upon his breastplate. Yet he was not old; the flaxen beard was still too young to have felt shears, his lightly sun-tanned skin was smooth and fair, his sea-blue eyes were clear and youthful. He glanced up at the star-flecked heaven, then drew the cloak about him.

"The Dragon marches low upon the skies," he muttered, " 'tis time I set forth on my journey if I would reach the homeland ere the winter tempests howl again."

The road was thick with travelers, mostly peasants on their way to market, for the day began with sunrise, and bartering would start within an hour. Hucksters of every sort of article, fanciful as well as necessary, pressed along the way, tugging at halters, now entreating, now berating their pack animals to greater speed. A patrol of soldiers passed and their decurion raised his hand in greeting.

"*Salve*, Claudius! Art thou truly going back to that cold land of thine? By Pluto, I am sorry that thou leavest us; many is the silver penny I have won by betting on those fists of thine, or on thy skill at swordplay!"

The Northman smiled amusedly. Though he had been among the Romans since before his beard was sprouted, their rendering of his simple Nordic name of Claus to Claudius had never failed to rouse his laughter.

"Yea, Marcus, I am soothly gone this time. Five years and more I have served Herod's whim, and in that time I've learnt the art of war as few can know it. With sword and axe and mace, or with bare hands or cestus have I fought until methinks I've had my fill of fighting. Now I go back to till my father's acres, perchance to go a-viking if the spirit moveth me, but hereafter I fight for mine own gain or pleasure, not to the humor of another."

"The gods go with thee, then, Barbarian," the Roman bade. " 'Twill be a long time ere we see thy match upon the sands of the arena."

A rambling, single-streeted village fringed the highway, and at the trickling fountain where the women came to fill their jars the wayfarer stopped to scoop up a sup of tepid water in his hand. The sun was up six hours and the little square around the spring should have been alive with magpie-chattering women and their riotously noisy children; but the place was like a city of the dead.

Silence thick as dust lay on the white sun-bitten road, utter quiet sealed the wayside houses with the silence of a row of tombs. Then, as he looked about in wonderment, Claus heard a thin-drawn, piping wail: *"Ai-ai-ai-ai!"* the universal cry of mourning in the East. *"Ai-ai-ai-ai!"*

He kicked aside the curtain at the doorway and looked into the darkness of the house. A woman crouched cross-legged on the earthen floor, her hair unbound, her gown ripped open to expose her bosom, dust on her brow and cheeks and breast. Quiet, but not sleeping, a baby lay upon her knees—a baby boy, and on the whiteness of his little body flowered a crimson wound. Claus recognized it—a gladiator knew the trade mark of his calling!—a sword-cut. Half a hand's span long it was, and ragged at the edges, sunk so deep into the baby flesh that the glint of white

[14]

breastbone showed between its gaping bloody lips.

"Who did this thing?" the Northman's eyes were hard as fjord-ice, and a grimness set upon his bearded lips like that they wore when he faced a Capadocian netman in the circus. "Who hath done this thing to thee, Woman?"

The young Jewess looked up from her keening. Her eyes were red and swollen with much weeping, and tears had made small rivulets in the dust smearing her face, but even in her agony she showed some traces of her wonted beauty.

"The soldiers," she replied between breath-breaking sobs. "They came and went from house to house as the Angel of the Lord went through the land of Egypt, but we had no blood to smear our lintels. They came and smote and slew; there is not a man-child left alive in all the village. Oh, my son, my little

[15]

son, why did they do this thing to thee, thou who never did them any harm? Oh, woe is me, my God hath left me comfortless; my firstborn, only son is slain—"

"Thou liest, woman!" Claus's words rang sharp as steel. "Soldiers do not things like this. They war with men; they make no war on babes."

The mother rocked her body to and fro and beat her breast with small clenched fists. "The soldiers did it," she repeated doggedly. "They came and went from house to house, and slew our sons—"

"Romans?" Claus asked incredulously. Cruel the Romans were at times, but never to his knowledge had they done a thing like this. Romans were not baby-killers.

"Nay, the soldiers of the King. Romans only in the armor that they wore. They came marching into town, and—"

[16]

"The soldiers of the King? Herod's?"

"Yea, Barbarian. King Herod, may his name be cursed for evermore! Some days agone came travelers from the East who declared a king was born among the Jews, and Herod, fearing that the throne might go to him, dispatched his soldiery throughout the coasts of Bethlehem to slay the sons of every house who had not reached their second year."

"Thy husband—"

"Alas, I am a widow."

"And hast thou store of oil and meal?"

"Nay, my lord, here is only death. *Ai-ai-ai—*"

Claus took some copper from his pouch and dropped it into the woman's lap beside the little corpse. "Take this," he ordered, "and have done unto the body of thy babe according to thy custom."

"The Lord be gracious unto thee, Barbarian. To thee and all thy house, for that thou takest pity on the widow in her sorrow. The Lord of Abraham, of Isaac and of Jacob—"

"Let be. What is thy name?"

"Rachael, magnificence; and may the Lord of Israel give favor unto—"

Claus turned away and left the weeping woman with her dead.

The waxing moon rode high above the grove where Claus lay bundled in his cloak. Occasionally from the denser thickets came the chirp of bird or squeak of insect, but otherwise the night was silent, for robbers roamed the highway after dark, and though the soldiers of the Governor kept patrol the wise man stayed indoors until the sun had risen. But the hardiest highwayman would stop and give the matter sober second thought ere he attacked a sworded giant, and the nearest inn was several miles away; also a journey of a thousand

miles and more lay between the Northman and his home, and though his wallet bulged with gold saved from his
years spent as a hired fighter in the
Tetrarch's barracks, it behooved him to
economize. Besides, the turf was sweet
to smell, which the caravansaries were
not, and the memory of the widow
woman's murdered son had set a canker
in his brain. It were better that he had
no traffic with his fellow men for several hours.

The broken rhythm of a donkey's
hoofs came faintly to him from the highway. The beast walked slowly, as though
tired, and as if he who led it were
also weary and footsore, yet urged by
some compulsion to pursue his journey
through the night.

"By Thor!" mused Claus, "they are a
nation of strange men, these Jews. Always disputing, ever arguing, never fal-
tering in their lust for gold; yet withal

they have a spirit in them like no other people has. Should their long-sought Messiah finally come, methinks that all the might of Rome would scarcely be enough to stop them in their—"

The hail came piercingly, mounting to a sharp crescendo, freighted with a burden of despair. "Help—help—we be beset by robbers!"

Claus smiled sardonically. "So eager to be early at tomorrow's market that he braves the dangerous highway after dark, and when the robbers set upon him—"

A woman's scream of terror seconded the man's despairing hail, and Claus bounded from his couch upon the turf, dragging at the sword that hung between his shoulders.

A knot of spearmen clustered round a man and woman. From their crested helmets and bronze cuirasses he knew them to be soldiers in the livery of

Rome; by their hook-nosed faces he knew them for Syrians, Jewish renegades, perhaps, possibly Arabs or Armenians, for such composed the little private army which the Tetrarch kept for show, and to do the work he dared not ask the Roman garrison to do.

"Ho, what goes on here?" challenged Claus as he emerged from the grove. "What mean ye by molesting peaceful travelers?"

The decurion in command turned on him fiercely. "Stand back, Barbarian. We be soldiers of the King, and—"

"By Father Odin's Ravens, I care not if ye be Caesar's soldiers, I'll have your reason for attacking this good man and wife, or the sword sings its song!" Claus roared.

"Seize him, some of you," the decharch ordered. "We'll take him to the Tetrarch for his pleasure. The rest stand by, we have our task to do—give me thy baby, Woman!" He bared his sword and strode up to the woman seated on the ass, a sleeping baby in her arms.

And now the wild war-madness of his people came on Claus. A soldier sprang at him and thrust his lance straight at his face, but Claus's long sword clove through bronze spearhead and ash-wood stave, and left the fellow unweaponed before him. Then before his adversary could drag out his shortsword Claus thrust, and his blade pierced through the soldier's shield and through the arm behind it, and almost through the cuirassed body. The man fell with a gasping cry and three more soldiers leapt at Claus, heads low above their shields, their lances at rest.

"*Aie*, for the song of the sword, *aie* for the red blood flowing, *aie* for the lay Storm-Maidens sing of heroes and Valhalla!" chanted Claus, and as he sang he struck, and struck again, and his

[22]

gray-steel blade drank thirstily. Four soldiers of the Tetrarch's guard he slew before they could close with him, and when two others, rushing to attack him from behind, laid hands on him, he dropped his sword and, reaching backwards, took his adversaries in his arms as if he were some monstrous bear and beat their heads together till their helmets toppled off and their skulls cracked and they fell dead, blood rushing from their ears and noses. Now only four remained to face him, and he seized the double-bladed axe that dangled at his girdle and with a mighty shout leapt on his foes as though they had been one and he a score. His iron axe-blade clove through bronze and bullock-hide as though they had been parchment, and two more of the Tetrarch's guardsmen fell dead; the other two turned tail and fled from this avenging fury with the fiery wind-blown beard and long fair hair that streamed unbound upon the night wind. Then Claus stood face to face with the decurion.

"Now, sayer of great words and doer of small deeds, thou baby-killer, say, wilt thou play the man's game, or do I smite thee headless like the criminal thou art?" asked he.

"I did but do my duty, Barbarian," the decurion answered sulkily. "The great King bade us go through all this land and take the man-child of each house, if he were under two years old, and slay him. I know not why. A soldier's duty is to bear his orders out."

"Aye, and a soldier's duty is to die, by Odin's Twelve Companions!" Claus broke in. "Take this for Rachael's child, the widow woman's only son, thou eater-up of little helpless babes!" And he aimed an axe-blow at the decharch, and never in his years of fighting in the circus had Claus the Smiter smitten such a blow. Neither shield nor mail could stop it, for the axe-blade sheared through both as if they had been parchment, and the axe-edge fell upon the decharch's neck where neck and shoulder join, and cut through bone and muscle, and cleaving on bit deep into the decharch's breast until it split his very heart in two, and as the oak tree falls when fire from heaven blasts it, so fell the soldier of King Herod in the dust at Claus's feet, and lay there, quivering and lifeless.

Then Claus unloosed the thong that bound the axe-helve to his wrist and tossed the weapon up into the air so that it spun around, a gleaming circle in the silver moonlight, and as it fell he caught it in his hand again and tossed it up above the whispering treetops, and sang a song of victory as his fathers had sung since the days when Northmen first went viking, and he praised the gods of Valhalla: to Odin, Father of the Gods, and Thor the Thunderer, and to the beauteous *Valkyrior*, choosers of the valiant slain in battle, he gave full meed of praise, and on the bodies of his fallen foes he kicked the gray road dust, and spat on them and named them churls and nidderings and unfit wearers of the mail of men of war.

His frenzy wore itself to calm, and putting up his axe he turned to look upon the little family he had succored. The man stood by the donkey's head, holding the lead-strap in one hand and in the other a stout stick which seemed to have been chosen for the double purpose of walking staff and goad. He was some fifty years of age, as the gray that streaked his otherwise black beard attested, and he was dressed from neck to heels in a gown of somber-colored woolen stuff which from its freshness was evidently the ceremonial best that

[26]

he was wont to wear on Sabbath to the synagogue. A linen turban bound his head, and before his ears the unshorn locks of "David-curls" hung down each side his face. His clothes and bearing stamped him as a countryman or villager, yet withal there was that simple dignity about him which has been the heritage of self-respecting poverty since time began.

Unmindful of the battle that had taken place so near it, the donkey cropped the short grass at the roadside in somnolent content, indifferent alike to war's alarms and the woman seated on the cushioned pillion strapped to its back. The woman on the ass was barely past her girlhood, not more than fifteen, Claus surmised as he looked appreciatively at her clear-cut lovely features. Her face was perfect oval, her skin like ivory, more pale than fair, her features were exquisite in their purity of outline; a faultless nose, full, sweetly-curving lips that had the indescribably lovely red of doves' feet, large eyes as blue as the ocean of Claus's homeland and, in harmony with all, a flood of golden hair which in the style permitted Jewish brides fell unconfined beneath her veil down to the pillion upon which she sat. Her gown was blue, as was her over-mantle, and a veil and wimple of white linen framed her features to perfection. Against her breast she held a tiny infant bound round and round in Jewish fashion with layer on layer of swaddling-clothes, and a single glance showed that the mother's beauty and sweet purity were echoed in the baby's face.

"We are beholden to you, sir," the man thanked Claus with simple courtesy. "Those men were seeking our son's life. Only last night the Angel of the Lord forewarned me in a dream to take

[28]

the young child and its mother and flee from Nazareth to Egypt, lest the soldiers of King Herod come upon us unawares. I hear that they have murdered many little ones whose parents had not warning from the Lord."

"Thou heard'st aright, old man," Claus answered grimly, thinking of the widow woman's son. "Back in the village yonder is the sound of lamentation. Rachael weeps for her dead and will not be comforted. Howbeit," he looked disdainfully upon the bodies in the road, "meseemeth I have somewhat paid the debt your kinsmen owed these murdering dogs."

"Alas," the traveler returned, "you have put your life in jeopardy for us, sir. After this there is a price upon your head, and Herod will not rest until he nails you to a cross for all to see the vengeance of the King."

"Sayest thou?" Claus laughed, but not

with mirth. "Methinks the sword will sing its song and many more like these will journey to the storm-land ere they hang me on the doom tree."

The blue eyes of the woman were on him as he spoke, and he stopped abashed. Never in the score and two years of wild life that had been his had Claus the Northman, Claus the gladiator, Claus the champion, felt a gaze like hers. He had a feeling of unworthiness, a sense that he stood in the presence of some being from another sphere, a sure and certain knowledge that this woman differed from all other women in the world.

"Your baby, Mistress," he said awkwardly, "may I look upon its face ere I go my ways? 'Tis something to have saved a little child from murderers' steel —a pity 'tis I was not in the village to save Widow Rachael's child as well."

The woman raised the infant in her

arms and the little boy's blue eyes were fixed on Claus. The Northman took a forward step to stroke the baby's smooth pink cheek, then, as if it had been a wall of stone that stopped him, halted where he stood. For a voice was speaking to him, or, rather, it was no mortal voice that spake, but a sound that touched his ears, yet seemed to come from nowhere.

"Claus, Claus," the softly modulated voice proclaimed, "because thou hast done this for me and risked thy life and freedom for a little child, I say that never shalt thou taste of death until thy work for me is finished."

Now though the infant's lips moved not, Claus knew the words proceeded from him. At first he was astonished, even frightened, for the world he knew was peopled with strange spirit-beings, all of whom were enemies to man. Yet as he looked into the baby boy's blue eyes, so calm, so knowing for an infant's, he felt his courage coming back, and made answer as was fitting when addressing a magician of more than usual power.

"Lord *Jarl*," he said, "I would not live always. There comes a time when arm grows weak and sight grows dim, however strong and brave the heart may be, and man is no more able to take part in the man's game. Say, rather, Lord, that I may die with sword or axe in hand and the wild war-shout in my mouth, in the full vigor of my manhood, and while the crimson tide of battle runs full-spate. Let it be that Odin's beauteous daughters deem me worthy to be taken from the battlefield and borne aloft to that Valhalla where heroes play the sword-game evermore."

"Not so, my Claus. Thou who hast put thy life in forfeit for the safety of a little child hast better things in store for thee.

When the name of Odin is forgot, and in all the world there is none to do him reverence, thy name and fame shall live, and laughing, happy children shall praise thy goodness and thy loving-kindness. Thou shalt live immortally in every childish heart so long as men shall celebrate my birthday."

"I shall live past *Ragnavok?*"

"*Ragnavok* is come, Claus. The old gods die, the fires upon their altars sink to whitened ashes and the voices of their worshippers grow weak, but thou shalt live so long as gleeful children praise thy name at the season of winter solstice."

"Then I shall be a mighty hero?"

"A hero to be held in loving memory by every man who ever was a child."

"Lord *Jarlkin,* I think thou art mistaken. Rather would I die with the sword-song in my ears and the din of battle for a dirge, but if thou speakest sooth, why, then, a man follows his star, and where mine leads I go."

Then Claus unsheathed his sword and flourished it three times above his head and finally brought its point to rest upon the road, for thus did heroes of the Northland pay respect to their liege lords.

The father cried out in afright when he heard the gray sword whistle in the air, but the mother looked on calmly, nor did she seem to marvel when the Northling spake in heathen language to her infant, as though he answered to unspoken words.

So Claus bade them safe faring on their way to Egypt land, and turned to face him toward the North Star and the homeward road.

II. The Road to Calvary

*L*UCIUS *PONTIUS PILATE,*
Procurator of Judea, leant across the
parapet and looked down at the night-
bound city. Lights blossomed here and
there among the flat-roofed houses;
now and then the clatter of mailed hoofs
was heard upon the cobblestones; almost incessantly there came the roar
of jostling, fractious crowds. Jerusalem

was crowded to the bursting point; for days the people had been streaming through the Joppa Gate, for a great feast was in preparation—these Jews were always celebrating either feast or fast—and the police power of his legionaries had been put upon its mettle.

"A turbulent and stiff-necked people these, my Claudius," the Governor addressed the tall blond-bearded man who stood three paces to his left and rear. "Ever disputing, always arguing and bickering, everlastingly in tumult of some sort. But yesterday when the troops marched from the citadel with the Eagles of the Legion at their head a band of townsmen stoned them, crying out that they bore graven images through the Holy City's streets. It seems they hold it a sin to make the simulacrum of anything that walks or flies or swims. A stubborn, narrow-minded lot, methinks."

"Aye, Excellence, a stubborn and rebellious lot," the first centurion agreed.

The Procurator laughed. "None knows it better than thyself, my Claudius. Thou wert here among them aforetimes, in the days of the great Herod, I've been told. How comes it that thou'rt here again? Dost like the odor of this sacred city of the Hebrews?"

The bearded soldier smiled sardonically. "I served King Herod as a gladiator a tricennium ago," he answered. "When my period of service was expired I found myself without a scar or wound, and with a wallet stuffed with gold. I told the praetor I would fight no more for hire, and set out for my northern home, but on my way—" He stopped and muttered something which the Procurator failed to catch.

"Yes? On the way—" the Roman prompted.

"I became embroiled with certain soldiers of the King who sought to do a little family violence. Herod swore a vengeance on me, and I was hunted like a beast from wood to desert and from desert to mountain. At last I sought the shelter which so many hunted men have found, and joined the legions. Since then I've followed where my star —and army orders—led, and now once more I stand within these city walls, safe from the vengeance of King Herod's heirs."

"And right glad am I that thou art here," Pilate declared. "This is no sinecure I hold, my Claudius. I have but a single legion to police this seething country, and treason and rebellion lift their heads on every side. Do I do one thing, the Jews cry out against me for that I have trespassed on some rite or custom which they hold in veneration. Do I do the other, again they howl to heaven that the iron heel of Rome oppresses them. By Jupiter! had I a dozen legions more—nay, had I but a single legion more of men like thee, my Claudius—I'd drive this mutinous rabble at the lance point till they whined like beaten dogs for mercy!" He gazed down at the city for a time in moody silence, then:

"What talk is this I hear of one who comes from Galilee claiming to be King of the Jews? Think ye it bodes sedition? Had they but a leader they could rally to I doubt not we should soon be fighting for our lives against these pestilent Judeans."

"I do not think we need fear insurrection from that quarter, Excellence," the soldier answered. "I saw this teacher when he came into the city but four days agone. Milk of mein he was, and very meek and humble, riding an ass's colt, which was a good sign, for

[41]

the Jews have a tradition that when kings go forth to war they bestride horses, but when they go in peace they use an ass for mount. I think he is a prophet rather than a priest or king, for afterwhiles he went into the temple, and instead of making sacrifices preached unto the people, bidding them to live as brethren, fear God, honor the King, and render unto Caesar that which is his."

"Ha, sayest thou? I had feared otherwise. Caiaphas, the chief priest, tells me he foments sedition, and urges that I throw him into prison or give him over to be crucified as one who preaches treason to the Empire."

"A priest's word—" the centurion began, the Governor laughed as he completed the vulgar proverb.

"I know. A priest's word, the laughter of fools and the anger of apes are alike to be regarded with contempt.

[42]

Natheless. . . ." He paused in pensive silence.

"Caiaphas!" the big centurion pursed his lips as though to spit. "That fatted swine! No wonder his religion bids him to refrain from pig's flesh. Were he to eat of it he would be a cannibal!"

Pilate nodded somberly. His quarrel with the high priest was one of long standing, and one in which the victories were even. Caiaphas had on occasion sent appeal to Rome, subtly intimating that unless the Governor yielded some disputed point there would be danger of rebellion. Word came back to Pilate that the Caesar held him personally responsible for conditions in Judea, and that in case of revolution his would be the blame. Thus the high priest triumphed in some controversies. On the other hand the Governor had advantage in that appeal in criminal cases and matters of taxation lay with him, and by asserting this authority he would often bend the prelate to his will.

"I would we had another pontifex," he mused. "One more pliant to suggestion than this sacerdotal fool who rules their priestly council."

The jingling clink of metal sword sheath on mailed kilts sounded as a legionary hurried out upon the roof, halted and saluted, then handed Claudius a scroll. The chief centurion returned the military salutation and in turn delivered the rolled missive to the Procurator.

"By Pluto's beard," swore Pilate as he broke the seal and read the message by the light of a small lanthorn set upon the parapet, "it comes sooner than we thought, my Claudius! Caiaphas has taken custody of this self-styled King of Jewry, tried him on a charge of blasphemy and treason before the Sanhedrin and judged him worthy to be crucified.

Now he brings the case to me on high petition. What are we to do?"

"Why, kick the fat pig squealing back to his sty, Excellence. None but Rome has jurisdiction in such cases. Caiaphas can no more condemn a man to death than he can don the toga of Imperial authority—"

"Aye, thou hast said it. But therein lies our difficulty, and our danger. I alone, as Procurator, can mete out sentence of death, but if these priests and their paid underlings should rouse the louse-bit rabble to rebellion we have not troops enough to put it down. Furthermore, should insurrection come, Rome is like to have my life. True, I am sent out here to govern and to rule, but chiefly to collect the tax. A people in rebellion pays no tribute to the throne. Come, Claudius, my toga. Let us hear what harm this uncrowned king hath done the state."

A murmur like a storm wind in the treetops filled the hall of audience. In the brilliant light of flambeaux double files of praetorian guardsmen stood at stiff attention as the Procurator took his seat upon the ivory and purple chair of state. Well forward in the hall, before the dais, stood Caiaphas with Simeon and Annas to his right and left. A knot of temple guards—tawdry imitations of the Roman legionaries—grouped about their prisoner, a tall young man in white, bearded in the Jewish fashion, but so light of skin and fair of hair he seemed to bear no racial kinship to the swarthy men surrounding him.

"Hail, Procurator!" Meticulously Caiaphas raised his right hand in the Roman fashion, then bowed with almost fawning oriental obsequiousness. "We come to you for confirmation of the sentence we have passed upon this blasphemer and traitor to the Empire."

[46]

Pilate's salutation was the merest lifting of the hand. "The blasphemy is your affair, priest," he answered shortly. "What treason hath he wrought?"

"He hath proclaimed himself a king, and if thou dost not find that treason, then thou art not Caesar's friend!"

"Art thou in very truth King of the Jews?" the Governor turned curious eyes upon the prisoner.

"Sayest thou this thing of me, or did others tell thee of it?" the young man answered.

"Am I a Jew?" the Procurator asked. "Thy own nation and thy chief priests have brought thee unto me for judgment. What hast thou done?"

There came no answer from the prisoner, but the murmuring outside grew ominous. A mob had gathered at the entrance and the guards were having trouble holding it in check.

Again the Procurator challenged. "Art

thou in truth a king, and if so, of what kingdom?"

"Thou hast said it. To this end was I born, and for this cause came I into the world, that I should bear witness to the truth. . . ."

"What is truth?" the Governor mused. "Myself have heard the sages argue long about it, but never have I found two who agreed on it. Claudius!" he turned to the centurion who stood behind his chair.

"Excellence!"

"I am minded to put these men to the test. Go thou to the dungeons and bring the greatest malefactor thou canst find into the hall. We shall see how far this bigotry can go."

As the soldier turned to execute the order the Governor faced the chief priest and his satellites. "I will have him scourged, then turn him free," he pronounced. "If he hath transgressed your

[48]

laws the scourging will be punishment enough; as to the charge of treason, I find no fault in him."

Docilely the prisoner followed a decurion to the barrack room where the soldiers stripped his garments off and lashed him to a pillar, then laid a tracery of forty stripes upon his naked back.

"The King of Jews, is he?" laughed the decurion. "Why, by the glorious eyes of Juno, every king should have a crown to call his own, yet this one hath no crown at all. Ho, there, some of you, go make a fitting crown for Jewry's King!"

A chaplet of thorn-branch was quickly plaited and thrust upon the prisoner's head, and the long sharp spines bit deeply in his tender flesh, so that a jewel-like diadem of ruby droplets dewed his brow. Then another found a frayed and tattered purple robe which they laid on his bleeding shoulders. Finally a reed torn from a hearth-broom was thrust between his tight-bound wrists for sceptre, and thus regailed they set him on a table and bowed the knee to him in mock servility, what time they hailed him as Judea's new King.

Now some of the guards from the temple had come into the barrack room to watch the scourging, and one of them said to another, "This man's disciples claim he has worked wonders, making blind men see and lame men walk, aye, even raised corpses from the dead." And hearing this some of the others stepped behind the prisoner and struck him on his raw scourge-wounded back, then when he turned mild eyes on them demanded, "If thou art truly given power from God to know all things, say which of us it was that smote thee."

But the decurion had wearied of the cruel sport, so they brought him back and set him on the pavement between Pilate and the priests. "Behold the man!"

the Procurator bade. "Behold your King, O men of Judea!"

"We have no king but Caesar!" Caiaphas cried self-righteously. "This one hath declared himself a king, and whoso calls himself a king speaketh against Caesar!"

Meanwhile Claudius was hastening to the judgment hall with a miserable object. The man was of great stature, but so bowed with fetters that he could not stand erect. His clothing was in tatters, no second glance was needed to know he was a walking vermin-pasture; the members of the prison guard shrank from him, fending him away with their lance-butts lest the lice that swarmed his hair and garments get to them.

Then Pilate bade the prisoner from the dungeons stand before the priests, and motioned to the bound and thorn-crowned captive.

"It is your custom, men of Judea, that

[51]

at the Passover I release to ye a prisoner," said the Procurator. "Whom will ye, therefore, that I set at liberty, this convicted robber, doomed to die upon the gallows tree, or this one ye have called your king?"

"We have no king but Caesar!" shouted Caiaphas in rage. "Away with this one! Crucify him!"

"What, crucify your king?" the Procurator asked in mock astonishment.

The mob of temple hangers-on that had been carefully rehearsed by Caiaphas and his underlings—the money-changers from the forecourt and traffickers in sacrificial doves who had been driven from their stalls by the prisoner three days since—thundered a chorus: "Crucify him!"

"Water in a ewer and a napkin, Claudius," ordered Pilate, and when his aide returned he set the silver basin down before him and laved his hands

[52]

in the water and dried them on the linen napkin. "Bear ye witness, priests and people. I am innocent of the blood of this just man. See ye to it!" cried the Procurator as he handed ewer and towel back to Claudius.

The high priest smiled in his beard. Once more he had bent Pilate to his will. "His blood be on our heads and on our children's heads," he answered, and the chorus massed outside the judgment hall took up the savage paean of blood-guiltiness: "On our heads and on our children's! Crucify him!"

Lucius Pontius Pilate shrugged his shoulders. "I have done the best I could, my Claudius. Let him be led away to prison, and on the morrow have him taken with the other adjudged malefactors and crucified. My guard will have no part in it, but I would that you go with the execution party to make sure all is regularly done and"—his thin lips parted in a mocking, mirthless smile—"to put my superscription on the cross to which they hang him. By Neptunus his trident, the same nails that pierce his members are like to prick the vanity of Caiaphas, methinks!" He chuckled softly to himself as if he relished some keen jest.

The procession to the execution hill or "Place of Skulls" began at dawn, for crucifixion was a slow death, and the morrow being Sabbath it was not lawful that the malefactors be left alive to profane the sacred day with their expiring groans. The crowds assembled in the city to keep Passover lined the Street of David and gathered at the alley-heads to watch the march of the condemned, making carnival of the occasion. Sweet-meat vendors and water-sellers did a thriving business with the merrymakers, and one or two far-sighted merchants who had come with panniers of rotten fruit and vegetables found ready market for their wares; for everyone enjoyed the sport of heaving offal at the condemned as they struggled past beneath the burden of their crosses.

Claudius did not go with them. The Procurator rested late that morning and there were routine matters to engage his time when he had finished at the bath. The sun was several hours high when a scrivener from the secretariat came into the *officium* with the *titulus* the Governor had dictated, engrossed on stiffened parchment. Pilate smiled with grim amusement as he passed the sheet to Claudius.

"Take thou this unto the place of execution, and with thine own hand fix it over the young Prophet's head," he ordered. " 'Twill give Caiaphas and his plate-lickers something fresh to whine about."

The centurion glanced at the scroll. In letters large enough for those who walked to read yet not be forced to slacken pace or strain their eyes is proclaimed:

IESVS NAZARENVS
REX IVDAEORVM

Which was to say: "This is Jesus (for such was the forename that the young Prophet bore) King of the Jews." Not only in Latin, but in Hebrew and Greek as well was the legend writ, that all who passed the place of crucifixion, whatever tongue they spake, might read and understand.

"They have prated long about a king who shall sweep away the power of Rome," the Procurator smiled. "Let them look upon him now, gibbeted upon a cross. By Jupiter, I would that I might see that fat priest's face when he reads my superscription!"

Three crosses crowned the bald-topped hill when Claudius reached the place of crucifixion. On two of them hung burly robbers, nailed by hands and feet, supported by the wooden peg or sedule set like a dowel in the upright beam between their legs, that their bodies might not sag too much or fall down from the gallows if their hands tore loose from the nails with their weight. In the center, spiked upon the tallest cross, hung the young Prophet, his frailer body already beginning to give way beneath the dreadful torment it endured. A decurion set a ladder up beside the cross, and armed with nail and hammer Claudius mounted quickly and fixed the placard to the upright beam above the bowed head of the dying man.

A thin, high, nickering cry of mixed astonishment and rage sounded as the legend on the card appeared. "Not that!" screamed Caiaphas as he put his hand up to his throat and rent his splendid priestly robe. "Not that, centurion! Yon superscription labels this blasphemer with the very title that he claimed, and for claiming which he now hangs on the gallows. Take down the card and change it so it reads that he is not our king, but that he claimed the kingly title in despite of Caesar!"

There was something almost comic in the priests' malevolence as they fairly gnashed their teeth in rage, and Claudius with the fighting man's instinctive contempt for politicians grinned openly as he replied, " 'Twere best you made complaint to Pilate, Priest. What he has written he has written, nor do I think that he will change yon title for all your whining grumble."

"Caesar shall hear of this!" the wrathful high priest snarled. "He shall be told how Pilate mocked our people and incited them to riot by labeling a hanged malefactor our King—"

Claudius turned abruptly to the centurion commanding the execution squad. "Clear away this rabble," he directed. "Must we be pestered by their mouthings?"

From the figure on the central cross a low moan came: "I thirst."

Claudius took a sponge and dipped it in the jar of sour wine and myrrh that stood beside him on the ground. He put it on a lance and held it to the sufferer's lips, but the poor weak body was too far spent to drink. A shudder ran through it, and with a final flash of strength the Prophet murmured: "It is finished. Father, into Thy hands I commend my spirit." A last convulsive spasm, and the thorn-crowned head fell forward on the shoulder. All was over.

"We had best be finishing our work," the execution squad's commander said phlegmatically. "These priests are set on mischief and we'll have a riot on our hands if one of these should live till sundown." He motioned to a burly executioner who picked up a sledge and methodically went about the task of smashing the suspended felons' arm- and leg-bones.

"Nay, by Father Odin's Ravens, thou shalt not break the good young Prophet's legs," Claudius declared as he snatched a guardsman's spear. "Let him die a man's death!" With the precision taught by years of training in the circus and on battlefield he poised the lance and drove the long bronze spearhead between the Prophet's ribs, sinking it deep into the heart. As he withdrew the point a stream of water mixed with blood gushed forth, and Claudius returned the soldier's spear. " 'Tis long since I have done that favor to a help-less man," he muttered as his memory flew back to his days in the arena when the blood-mad mob withheld the mercy sign and he had to thrust his sword or lance through his defeated adversary—often the man with whom he'd drunk and diced the night before. "By Friega's eyes," he added as he looked at the frail body stretched upon the cross, "he's beautiful! I've heard he called himself the Son of God, nor is it hard to credit. 'Tis no man, but a god who hangs on yonder gallows—Baldur the Beautiful, slain by foul treacheries!"

A ringing sounded in his ears like the humming of innumerable bees, and through it he heard words, words in a voice he had not heard in more than thirty years, but he recognized it instantly. "Claus, thou tookest pity on a little child attacked by murderers in days agone; this day thy pity bade thee save a dying man from brutish violence. According to thy lights thou dealtest mercifully when thou thrust the spear into my side. Knowest thou not me, Claus?"

"Lord *Jarlkin!*" Claus turned and

gazed in wonder at the slight, wilted body pendent on the cross. "The little child whom I assisted on his way to Egypt land! What wouldst thou with thy liegeman, Lord? Did not my mercy-stroke drive true—is my work yet unfinished?" He put his hand out for the soldier's spear again, but:

"Thy work is not yet started, Claus. I will call and thou shalt know my voice when I have need of thee."

The soldiers of the guard and crowd of hang-jawed watchers at the execution ground were thunderstruck to see the Procurator's chief centurion draw himself up and salute the body on the gallows as though it were a tribune, or the Governor himself.

Dark clouds obscured the sun and menacing thunder mingled with the stabbing spears of lightning as Claus hastened through the Street of David on his way back to the Governor's palace. Once or twice there came a rumbling in the bowels of the earth and the solid ground reeled drunkenly. A rout of citizens fled past him, running aimlessly as ants from a disturbed anthill. Their frightened voices were high-pitched as those of terrified children. "O God of Our Fathers, wherefore hast Thou forsaken us? . . . The rocks are split in twain! . . . The temple veil is ripped apart! . . . 'Tis said the graves gape open and the sheeted dead come forth!"

"Siguna goes to drain her cup and Loki writhes beneath the sting of serpent venom," Claus muttered as he dug his heels into his horse's sides. It would not be comfortable in that narrow street when the fury of the earthquake began to shake the buildings down. A temblor retched the riven earth afresh, and an avalanche of broken tile and rubble slid into the roadway, almost blocking it.

Claus slid down from the saddle and gave his horse a smart blow on the flank. "Go thou, good beast, Thor see thee safely to thy stable," he bade, then took shelter by the blank-walled houses, dashing forward a few steps, then shrinking back again as spates of falling masonry cataracted overhead and fell crashing on the cobbles of the street.

"*Ai-ai-ahee!*" a woman's scream came knife-edged with terror. "Help me, for the love of God! Save me, or I perish! Have mercy, Master!"

The flicker of a lightning flash lit up the pitch-black night-in-day that swamped the narrow way, and by its quivering brightness Claus saw a woman's body lying in the roadway. A timber from a broken house had fallen on her foot, pinning her against the cobbles, and even as she screamed a fresh convulsion of the earth shook down a barrow-load of broken brick and

[64]

tile, scattering brash and lime dust over her. A stone fell clanging on his helmet as he rushed across the gloom-choked street, and a fragment of broken parapet crashed behind his heels as he leant to prize the timber off her ankle. She lay as limp as a dead thing in his arms as he dashed back to the shelter of a wall, and for a moment he thought he had risked his life in rescuing one beyond the need of succor, but as he laid her down upon the flagstones her great eyes came open and her little hands crept up to clasp themselves about his neck. "Art safe, my lord?" she asked.

"Aye, for the nonce, but we tempt the gods by staying here. Canst walk?"

"I'll try." She drew herself erect and took a step, but sank down with a moan. "My foot—'tis broken, I fear," she gasped. "Do thou go on, my lord. Thou hast done thy duty to the full already. 'Tis better one should die than two; nor is it meet that thou shouldst stay and risk thy life for me—"

"Be silent, Woman," he commanded gruffly. "Raise thy arms!"

Obediently she put her arms about his shoulders and he lifted her as though she were a child. Then, his cloak about his head to fend off falling fragments of the buildings, he darted from house to house until the narrow street was cleared and they came at length to a small open space.

It was lighter here, and he could see his salvage. She was a pretty thing, scarce larger than a half-grown child, and little past her girlhood. Slender she was, yet with the softly rounded curves of budding womanhood. Her skin, deep sun-kissed olive, showed every violet vein through its veil of lustrous tan. Her hands, as dimpled as a child's, were tipped with long and pointed nails on which a sheathing of bright goldleaf had been laid, so that they shone like tiny mirrors. Her little feet were gilt-nailed like her hands and innocent of sandals and painted bright with henna on the soles and heels and toes. On ankles, wrists and arms hung bangles of rose gold set thick with lapis-lazuli and topaz and bright garnet, while rings of the same precious metal hung from each ear almost to her wax-smooth shoulders. On fore and little fingers of each hand and on the great and little toe of each foot she wore rings of gold set with green zircon, and a diadem of gold in which gems flashed was circled round her brow, binding back the curling black locks which lay clustering round her face. Her small high breasts were bare, their nipples stained with henna, and beneath her bosom was a zone of golden wire from which a robe of sheer vermilion gauze was hung. Beneath this she wore baggy trousers of black net as fine-meshed as a veil. Ground antimony had been rubbed on her eyelids, and her full voluptuous lips were stained a brilliant red with powdered cinnabar.

He recognized her: one of the *hetaerae* from the house of love kept by the courtezan of Magdala before she turned from harlotry to follow the young Prophet they had crucified that morning. Her mistress gone, the girl had taken service as a dancer at Agrippa's court. He drew away a little. His clean-bred northern flesh revolted at the thought of contact with the little strumpet.

"What didst thou in the street?" he asked. "Were there so few to buy thy wares within the palace that thou must hawk them in the highway?"

"I—I came to see the Master," she sobbed softly. "I had the dreadful malady, and I sought His cure."

"Aye? And didst thou find it?"

[68]

"Yea, that did I. As He went by, all burdened with His gibbet, I called on Him and asked His mercy, and He did but raise the fingers of one hand and look on me, and behold—I am clean and whole again. See, is not my skin as fresh and clean as any maiden's?"

He moved a little farther from her, but she crept toward him, holding out her hands for him to touch. "Behold me, I am clean!" she whispered rapturously. "No more will I be shunned of men—"

"By this one thou wilt be," he broke in grimly. "What have I to do with thee and thy kind, Girl? The earthquake passes; it is safe for thee to walk the streets again. Get thee to thy business. Be gone."

"But my broken foot—I cannot walk. Wilt thou not help me to my place—"

"Not I, by Thor! Let the scented darlings of the palace see to that." He shook her clinging hands away and half rose to his feet when a voice—the well-remembered voice his inward ear had heard before—came to him:

"Despise her not. I have had mercy on her, and thou—and I—have need of her in the work ordained for thee. Claus, take her to thee."

He stood irresolute a moment, then: "I hear and obey, Lord," he answered and sank down again upon the turf. "How art thou called?" he asked the girl.

"Erinna, may it please your magnificence."

"A Greek?"

"Tyrian, my lord." She moved closer to him and rubbed her supple body against his breastplate with a gentle, coaxing manner. "They brought me over the bright water while I was still a child, and schooled me in the arts of love, and I am very beautiful and much

[70]

desired, but now I am all thine." She bowed her head submissively and put his hand upon it. "Thou didst battle with the earthquake for me, and rived me from its clutches; now I belong to thee by right of capture."

Claus smiled, a trifle wryly. "What need have I, a plain blunt soldier, for such as thou?"

"I am very subtle in the dance, my lord. Moreover, I can sing and play sweet music on the harp and flute and cymbals. Also, I am skilled in cookery, and when thou hast grown tired of me thou canst sell me for much gold—"

"Men of my race sell not their wives—"

"Wife? Saidst thou wife, my lord?" she breathed the word incredulously.

"Am I a Greek or Arab to have slave girls travel in his wake? Come, rouse thee up; we must to the palace where quarters can be found for thee until I take thee to mine own."

Tears streamed down the girl's face, cutting little channels in the rouge with which her cheeks were smeared, but her smile looked through the tear drops as the sun in April shines through showers of rain. "In very truth, He told my future better than I knew!" she cried ecstatically, and to Claus's utter consternation bent suddenly and pressed a fervid kiss upon his buskin.

"What charlatan foretold thy future?" he demanded, raising her and crooking an arm beneath her knees, for her broken foot was swelling fast, and walking was for her impossible.

"The Master whom they crucified— may swine make wallows of their mothers' graves! When I bowed me in the dust and begged Him to have pity on me, He looked at me and smiled, e'en though He trod the way to torture and to death and was borne down with the weight of His gallows. He told me, 'Woman, thy desire shall be unto thee.' I thought He meant that I was healed, but—" She flung both arms about her bearer's neck and crushed his face against the hemispheres of her small bosoms as she sighed rapturously.

"But what, wench?"

"I have seen thee from afar, my Claudius. Long have I watched thee and had pleasure in thy manly beauty. At night I used to dream that thou wouldst notice me, perchance come unto me, or even buy me for thy slave; but that ever I should bear the name of wife"—again her voice broke on a sigh, but it was a sigh of pure happiness—"that I, Erinna the *hetaerae*—"

"Thy Greek name likes me not," he interrupted.

"What's in a name, my lord? I'll bear whatever name thou givest me, and be happy in it, since 'tis given me by thee.

By Aphrodite's brows, I'll come like any dog whene'er thou callest me by such name as it may please thee to give me—"

"Let be this talk of dogs and slaves," he broke in testily. "Thou'lt be a wife and equal—aye, by Thor's Iron Gauntlets, and whoso fails to do thee honor shall be shorter by a head!"

Pilate's legion was recruited largely from Germanic tribesmen, and among these Claus found enough of his people to arrange a marriage ceremony like those of his homeland. Erinna's name was changed to Unna, and on the day they wed she sat in the bride's seat robed in modest white with a worked head-dress on her clustering black ringlets, a golden clasp about her waist and gold rings on her arms and fingers. The Northlings raised their drinking-skulls aloft and shouted *"Skoal!"* and *"Waes hael!"* to the bride and bridegroom, and clamored on their shields with sword

[74]

and axe. Then, when the feast was finished and the bride's cup had been drained, because her broken foot was not yet mended, Claus bore Unna in his arms to the bride's bed. Thus did Claudius the centurion, who was also Claus the Northling, wed a woman out of Tyre in the fashion of the Northmen.

Now talk ran through the city of Jerusalem that the Prophet whom the priests had done to death was risen from the dead. Men said that while His sepulchre was watched by full-armed guards an angel came and rolled away the stone and He came forth, all bright and glorious. And many were the ones who testified that they had seen Him in His resurrected flesh.

The priests and temple hangers-on cast doubt upon the story, and swore that whilst the guardsmen slept the Prophet's followers had come and stolen Him away, but Claus and Unna both believed. That Mary Magdalene who aforetime had been Unna's mistress swore she had seen Him in the garden by the tomb, and heard His voice and touched His solid flesh. Claus knew that soldiers under Pilate's orders did not sleep on duty. The Prophet's followers could no more have won through the guard to steal His body from the tomb than they could have rescued Him from a dungeon in the citadel.

"Said I not He was a god, e'en as He hanged upon the gallows tree?" asked Claus. "Baldur the Beautiful is He: Baldur the Fair cannot be holden by the gates of Hel; He is raised up again in their despite."

"He is indeed the Son of God, as Mary Magdalene said," Unna answered as she laid her cheek against her husband's breast. "He healed me of my

[76]

malady and gave me that which I desired above all things."

Claus kissed his newly married wife upon the mouth. "He said that I had need of thee, my sweetling," he whispered. "I knew it not, but He spake sooth. And," he added in an even softer tone, "He said likewise He had need of thee. We shall hear His call and answer Him whenever He shall please to summon us, though the summons come from lowest Niflheim."

III. The Long, Long Road

MEN grew old and grayed
and died in the service of Imperial
Rome, but neither death nor old age
came to Claus. His ruddy hair retained
its sheen, and when men who had joined
the legions as mere beardless youths
laid by the sword and sate them in the
ingle-nook to tell brave tales of battles
fought and won on field and sea he was
still instinct with youthful vigor. For

years he followed Pilate's fortunes, acting as his aide-de-camp and confidant, and when the aging Governor went from Palestine to Helvetia it was Claus who went with him as commander of his soldiery. When death at last came to his patron, Claus stood among the mourners and watched the funeral flames mount crackling from the pyre, then turned his face toward Rome, where men of valor still were in demand. As a tribune he went with Agricola to Britain and helped beat back the Picts and Scots and lay the first foundations of the great wall that still endures. He followed Aurelian to Palmyra, and, disdainful of the flaming pitch and Greek fire hurled down by the defenders, led the assaults on the city walls.

When the Emperor returned to Rome and rode in splendid triumph through the streets Claus walked behind the chariot drawn by four white stags in

which the conqueror rode and helped
Zenobia, the captive Palmyrene Queen,
bear the golden fetters fixed upon her
wrists and neck, for she was fainting
from their burden, and it irked him to
see the great-hearted woman who had
dared dispute the might and majesty of
Rome borne down beneath the weight
of chains, though they were solid gold.

As commander of a legion he stood
with Constantine the Great at Malvian
Bridge when, beneath the emblem of
the once despised Cross, Maximian's
youthful son defeated old Maxentius
and won the purple toga of the Caesars.
With Constantine he sailed across the
Bosphorus and helped to found the
world's new capital at Byzantium.

Emperors came and went. The kingdom of the Ostrogoths arose in Italy and
strange bearded men who spoke barbarian tongues ruled in the Caesars' stead.
But though the olden land of Latium no

longer offered reverence to the Empire, it owed allegiance to the name of Him the priests had crucified so long ago in Palestine; for nowhere, save in the frozen fjords and forests of the farthest North and in the sun-smit deserts of the South, did men fail to offer prayer and praise and sacrifice to the Prophet who had come to save His people from their sins and had been scornfully rejected by their priests and leaders.

And now a mighty conflict arose between the Christians of the West and the followers of Mahound in the East; and Claus who knew the country round about Jerusalem as he knew the lines that marked his palms rode forth with Tancred and Count Raymond and Godfrey of Bouillon to take the Holy City from the Paynim's hands. With him rode the ever-faithful, thrice-beloved Unna, armed and mounted as a squire. Never since the morning of their marriage had

[84]

they been out of voice-call of each
other; for she had shared his life in
camp and field, marching with the
legions dressed in armor like a man, going to Byzantium when the New Empire
was founded, riding at his side across
the troubled continent of Europe when
the Old Empire broke to pieces and
little kings and dukes and princes set
their puny courts up in the midst of their
walled towns. Sometimes she cut her
long hair and went forth in male garb;
again, in those brief intervals of peace
when they dwelt at their ease in some
walled city, she let her tresses grow and
assumed woman's attire and ruled his
house with gentleness and skill as became the mate of one who rated the
esteem of prince and governor, for her
husband's fame at weaponry and sagac-
ity in war had won him great standing
among those who had need of strong
arms and wise heads to lead their sol-

diery and beat their foemen back.

Now Claus, with Unna fighting at his elbow as his squire, had assailed the walls when Godfrey and Count Eustace and Baldwin of the Mount leaped from the flaming tower and held the Paynim back till Tancred and Duke Robert broke Saint Stephen's Gate and forced their way into the Holy City; but when the mailed men rode with martial clangor through the streets and massacred the populace they took no part. In the half darkness of the mosque that stood hard by the ancient Street of David where aforetime the young Prophet had trod the *Via Dolorosa* they saw old Moslems with calm features watch their sons' heads beaten in with axe or mace and then in their turn submit to slaughter; it was the will of Allah, and *fi amam 'llah*—we are all in His protection. They heard the Paynim women beg and plead for mercy, saw Christian sword and pike rip open their soft bodies till their cries were stilled. They tried to stop the wanton killing and begged the men-at-arms and knights to stay their hands and show their helpless foemen clemency, whereat the wearers of the Cross turned on them with curses and swore they were no true and loyal lovers of the Prince of Peace.

But when the killing and the rapine ceased and men went forth to worship at the Holy Places Claus and Unna walked the city hand in hand, and their eyes were soft with memories. " 'Twas here we met, my love, doest thou remember?" Claus asked as they walked through David's Street, and Unna answered never a word, but her arms crept up around his neck as they had been the tendrils of a vine, and drew his face down to hers till her lips found his and clung as if they would weld flesh to flesh and never more be severed.

"And here He raised His hand and blessed them who did persecute Him," Unna told a group of gentlewomen who had come to make the pilgrimage to Calvary upon their knees. "And here He fainted underneath the burden of His gallows. . . ." But when the Frankish women heard her they would not heed, but hooted her away, for their chaplains who until that time had never seen Jerusalem had shown them where the Master trod, and sooth, the learned holy men knew more of sacred things than this wild woman of the camps who wore her hair at shoulder length and fared forth dight in hose and doublet like a man and swaggered it among the men-at-arms with a long sword at her thigh.

But when she told them that she knelt upon those very stones and watched Him bear the cross to Golgotha they shrank from her and named her witch and crossed themselves and called on every saint they knew for succor. And presently men came to take her. She fought like any leopardess and more than one armed man felt the sting of her steel. But they were twenty, she was one, so afterwhiles they bound her arms with cords and took her to the prison-house beneath the Templars' stables and swore that on the morrow they would burn her at a stake that all might see what fate befell a woman who spake blasphemy within the very confines of Jerusalem.

When she came not to their dwelling-place that night Claus was like a man made mad by those foul drugs the Paynims use to give them courage in the fight. And he went to the prison-house and smote the warders where they stood, so that they fled from him as from a thing accursed, and with his mighty axe he brake the heavy doors that shut her in, and they went forth from that place and took horse and rode until they reached the sea, where they took ship and sailed away. And no man durst stand in their way, for the flame of Northern lightnings burned in Claus's eyes, and he raged like a wild berserker if any bade them stand and give account of whence they came and where their mission led them.

The years slipped swiftly by like rapid rivers running in their courses, and Claus and Unna rode the paths of high adventure. Sometimes they rested in the cities, but more often they were on the open road, or fighting in the armies of some prince or duke or baron, and always fame and fortune came to them. But they could not abide in any one place long, for betimes they came in conflict with the theologians, for when these heard them speak of the Great Teacher as though they had beheld Him in the flesh they sought to

have them adjudged witch and warlock, and so great was these men's
power that had they not been fleet of
foot and strong of arm they were like to
have been burnt a dozen times and
more.

As they passed through Genève on
their way to Italy where Claus had business with the duke of a city, they saw a
great throng gathered as for holidaying,
and presently they saw a man led forth
to die by fire. It was no roaring holo-
caust they kindled at his feet, but a
small fire of faggots, so that the flames
licked slowly at his searing flesh and
stripped it from his bones as great
cat-beasts lap meat with roughened
tongues. As the victim's screams were
mingled with the crackling of the flames
and jeers of the multitude Unna hid her
face against her husband's arm, and
Claus swore underneath his breath as
soldiers have at needless suffering since
time was young. But the crowd drank

in the spectacle avidly, and he was minded of another mob that gathered round a cross on Golgotha in days gone by.

"Who was that one, friend, and what was his great crime that he should die thus painfully?" Claus asked a lean man in the drab stuff gown and shovel hat that marked him as a pastor of the Reformed Faith.

"He was the Spaniard Serveto," answered the ecclesiastic. "He was denounced by our good leader, Maître Jean Calvin, for blaspheming the truth, and richly hath he deserved death at the stake."

Now Claus remembered Pilate's question asked so long ago, and in his turn repeated: "What is truth?"

Whereat the other told him, "Truth is as we preach it; all else is heresy and lies, and merits death in this world and damnation in the next!"

"Now, by the Iron Gloves of Thor," swore Claus when he heard this, "me-seems the very milk of human kindness hath been curdled into clabber by these men. 'Twas Caiaphas and Annas and their ilk who hanged the Master on the cross because they said He blasphemed truth; today the men who call themselves His ministers and servants roast their fellows at the stake for the same reason! It matters not at whose altar he serves, the priest is still a priest and changeth not."

One Yuletide Claus and Unna lodged in a small city by the Rhine. The harvest was not plentiful that year, and want and famine stalked the streets as if an enemy laid siege to the town. The feast of Christmas neared, but in the burghers' houses there was little merriment. Scarce food had they to keep starvation from their bellies, and none at all to make brave holiday upon the Birthday of the Lord.

And as they sate within their house Claus thought him of the cheerless faces of the children of the town, and as he thought he took a knife and block of wood and carved the semblance of a sleigh the like of which the people used for travel when the snows made roads impassable for wheels or horsemen.

When Unna saw his handiwork she laughed aloud and clipt him in her arms and said, "My husband, make thou more of those, as many as the time 'twixt now and Christmas Eve permits! We have good store of sweetmeats in our vaults, and even figs from Smyrna and sweet dried grapes from Cyprus, Sicily and Africa, besides some quantity of barley sugar. Do thou carve out the little sleighs and I will fill them to the brim with comfits; then on the Eve of Christ His Birthday we'll go amongst the poorest of the townsfolk and leave little gifts upon their doorsteps, that on the morrow when the children wake they shall not have to make their Christmas feast on moldy bread and thin meat broth."

The little sleighs piled up right swiftly, for it seemed to Claus his fingers had a nimbleness and skill they never had before, and he whittled out the toys so fast that Unna was amazed and swore his skill at wood-carving was great as with the sword and axe; whereat he laughed and whittled all the faster.

It was bitter cold on Christmas Eve, and the members of the night watch hid themselves in doorways or crept into cellars to shield them from the snow that rode upon the storm wind's howling blast; so none saw Claus and Unna as they made their rounds, leaving on each doorstep of the poor a little sleigh piled high with fruits and sweets the like of which those children of that northern clime had never seen before. But one small lad whose empty belly would not let him sleep looked from his garret window and espied the scarlet cloak Claus wore, for Claus went bravely dressed as became a mighty man of valor, and one who walked in confidence with princes. And the urchin marveled much that Claus the mighty captain of whose feats men spoke with bated breath should stop before his doorstep. But anon he slept, and when he waked he knew not if it were a dream he dreamt, or if he had seen Claus pass through the storm all muffled in his crimson cloak.

But when the church bells called the folk to prayer and praise next morning and the house doors were unbarred, the people found the sleighs all freighted with their loads of comfits on their thresholds, and great and loud was the rejoicing, and children who had thought

[96]

that Christmas was to be another day of fasting clapped their hands and raised their voices in wild shouts of glee. And Claus and Unna who went privily about the streets saw their work and knew that it was good, and their hearts beat quicker and their eyes shone with the tears of happiness, for that they had brought joy where sorrow was before, and they clasped each other by the hand and exchanged a kiss like lovers when their vows are new, and each swore that the other had conceived the scheme and each denied it; so in sweet argument they got them to the minster, and then went to their house where their Christmas feast of plump roast goose was sweeter for the thought of joy they had brought to the children of the town.

But when the clergy of the town were told about the miracle of fruits and sweets that came unmarked upon the doorsteps of the poor they were right wroth, and swore this was no Christian act, but the foul design of some fell fiend who sought to buy men's souls away by bribing them with Satan's sweetmeats.

The lad whose waking eyes had seen Claus in his scarlet mantle told his tale, and all the poor folk praised him mightily as one who had compassion on the sufferings of childhood, but the churchmen went to the *Burggraf* of the city saying, "Go to, this man and his wife foment rebellion; they have sought to buy the people's loyalty away by little gifts made to their children."

"Why, as to that," the *Burggraf* answered, "meseems it is a good and kindly thing they did. Indeed, they have put shame on us, sith we of our abundance gave no alms to those who hungered. These be stern times for poor men, good your reverences."

When they heard this the clerics murmured one to another, and finally put forth the saintly pastor of the High Minster to make answer for them all. He was a very learned man and skilled in disputation. He knew how many angels could dance on the point of a needle, and whether angels traveling from one place to another passed through intervening space. Moreover, he was deeply versed in demonology, and could smell wizardry or witchcraft featly as the beagle scents the cony, so when he spake he spake with great authority, and thus he spake to the *Burggraf*:

"The poor we have with us alway. Did not the blessed Master say as much, aye, and wrathfully rebuke His disciples who would have had Mary Magdalene's embrocation sold to buy bread for them? It is no work of merit to give bread unto the poor. If it were Heaven's will that all men should be fed then we should have no poor, but it is stated most explicitly that the poor we shall have with us alway. It is the well-considered thought of this most reverend company that it is little less than a defiance of divine purpose to alleviate their condition. If wise all-seeing Heaven had not willed them to be poor they had not been so, but sith their poverty is obviously by divine decree, whoso maketh them less poor, even though it be by giving them no more than a dry crust, thwarts Heaven's will, and is therefore no better than a contemnor of the Holy Gospel. And as all wizardry is a species of heresy, it follows as the night the day that heresy is also a form of witchcraft, and Holy Scripture saith expressly, 'Thou shalt not suffer a witch to live.'

"Look ye to it, then. If you permit this man and woman, who are no better than a witch and warlock, to remain at large you are no friend of true religion, nor of the *Landgrave* from whom you hold this city as a fief. *Dixi.*"

"Amen," said all the others. "Our reverend brother speaketh most sound doctrinal advice, which you will take to heart if you be truly righteous."

So the *Burggraf* would have put them into prison on a charge of witchcraft and treason, but the townsmen came to them and warned them of the net the churchmen wove; so they escaped before the men-at-arms came clamoring at their door and fled across the winter snows. Behind them swept a raving tempest, so that those who sought to follow were engulfed in drifting snows and lost their tracks upon the road, and finally turned round and fought their way back to the city with the tidings they had surely perished in the storm.

Now presently their travels took them to the Baltic shores, and as they passed across the country of the Lappmen they came to a small valley ringed round with nine low hills, and no man durst go to that place, for 'twas said the little brown men of the land beneath the earth had power there and whoso met them face to face was doomed to be their servant always, and to slave and toil beneath the ground for evermore, because these people had no souls, but were natheless gifted with a sort of immortality so that they should live until the Judgment Day when they and all the great host of the olden gods should stand before the awful throne of the Most High and hear sentence of eternal torment.

But Claus and Unna had no fear of the aelf people or of any harm that they might do, for both of them wore crosses round their necks, and in addition each was girt with a long sword, and the great axe that had aforetime laid the mightiest foemen in the dust was hanged from Claus's saddle-bow.

So they bent their way among the haunted Nine Hills, and behold, as they rode toward the sea there came a great procession of the aelfmen bearing packs upon their backs and singing dolefully. "*Waes hael* to thee, small aelfmen," Claus made challenge, "why go ye sadly thus with chant of dole and drearihead?"

"Alack and well-a-day," the aelf King answereth, "we take our way to Niflheim, there to abide until the time shall come when we are sent to torment everlasting, for the folk whom we did help aforetime now cry out upon us and say we are devils and set no pan of milk or loaf of barley bread beside their doorstep for us; nor do they tell the tales their fathers told of kindly deeds done by the Little People, but only tales of terror and wickedness. For this we are no longer able to come out and play upon the earth's good face, neither dance and sing by moonlight in the

[103]

glades, and, worst of all, our human neighbors have no use for our good offices, but drive us hence with curse and chant and bell and book and candle."

Now Claus laughed long and loud mirthlessly when he heard this, for well was he reminded of the time when he and Unna had to flee for very life because they had done kindness to the poor, so he made answer: "Would ye then find it happiness to serve your human neighbors an ye could?"

"Aye, marry, that would we," the aelf King told him. "We be great artificers in both wood and stone and metal. There are no smiths like unto us, nor any who can fashion better things of crockery, and much would it delight our hearts to shape things for men's service and bestow them on the goodmen of the farms and villages and towns, but now they will have none of us or of our gifts. Why, to say a present is a fairy gift is to insult the giver in these days!"

Now as Claus listened to this plaint there came a ringing as of many bells within his ears and once again the voice he knew spake to him and he heard: "Claus, thou hast need of these small men. Take them with thee on the road that shall be opened to thy feet."

So Claus bespake the aelfmen's King and said: "Wouldst go with me unto a place of safety, and there work diligently to make things that children joy to have? If thou wilt do it I'll see that thy gifts are put into the hands of those who will take joy in them and praise thy name for making them."

"My lord, if thou wilt do this thing for us I am thy true and loyal vassal, now and ever, both I and all my people," swore the aelfmen's King. So on the fresh green turf he kneeled him down upon his knees and swore an oath of fealty unto Claus, acknowledging himself his vassal and vowing to bear true and faithful service unto him. Both he and all his host of tiny men pronounced the vow, and when they rose from off their knees they hailed Claus as their lord and leader.

Then from their treasure-store they brought a little sleigh no larger than the helm a soldier wears to shield his skull from sword-blows, and so cunningly contrived it was that it could stretch and grow until it had room for them all, both the aelf King and his host and Claus and Unna and their steeds as well.

And when they had ensconced them in the magic sleigh they harnessed to it four span of tiny reindeer no larger than the timid squeaking mice that steal forth in the night to forage in the farmer's kitchen, and at once these grew until they were as large as war-steeds, and with a shout the aelf King bade them go, and straightway they rose up into the air and drew the sleigh behind them, high above the heaving billows of the Baltic.

"Bid them ride until they have the will to stop," Claus ordered, and the aelf King did as he commanded, and presently, far in the frozen North where the light of the bridge Bifrost bears upon the earth the reindeer came to rest. And there they builded them a house, strong-timbered and thick-walled, with lofty chimneys and great hearths where mighty fires roared ceaselessly. And in the rooms about the great hall they set their forges up, and their kilns for baking earthenware and benches for wood-turning. And the air was filled with sounds of metal striking metal as cunning dwarfs beat toys of metal out while others of their company plied saw and knife and chisel, making toys of wood, and others still made dolls of plaster and chinaware and clothed them in small garments which artful aelfmen under Unna's teaching fashioned at the great looms they had built. And in the castle garth they set out groves of holly trees and oaks on which the mistletoe grew thick, for the holly's ruddy berry is the symbol of the drops of precious blood Christ shed for our redemption, and the pearly fruit of mistletoe is emblematic of His tears of compassion for our weakness, so both of them are fitting garniture for Christian homes at Yuletide.

When Christmas Eve was come again there was a heap of toys raised mountain-high, and Claus put them into the magic sleigh with wreaths of gleaming holly and white boughs of mistletoe and whistled to the magic reindeer and called them each by name, and off they sped across the bridge Bifrost where in the olden days men said the gods had crossed to Asgard. And so swiftly sped his eight small steeds, and so well his sleigh was stocked with toys that before the light of Christmas morning dawned there was a gift to joy the heart of every child laid on each hearth, and Claus came cloud-riding again unto his Northern home and there his company of cunning dwarfs and Unna the beloved waited.

Then they made a mighty feast and heaped the tables till they groaned beneath the weight of venison and salmon and fat goose, and the mead horns frothed and foamed, and song and laughter echoed from the high walls of the castle as they bid each other *skoal* and *waes hael* while they drank and drank again to childhood's happiness.

Long years ago Claus laid aside his sword, and his great axe gathers rust upon the castle wall; for he has no need of weapons as he speeds on his way to do the work foretold for him that night so long ago upon the road to Bethlehem.

Odin's name is but a memory, and in all the world none serves his altars, but

Claus is very real today, and every year ten thousand times ten thousand gleeful children wait his coming; for he is neither Claudius the gladiator nor Claus the mighty man of war, but Santa Claus, the very patron saint of little children. His is the work his Master chose for him that night two thousand years ago; his the long, long road that has no turning so long as men keep festival upon the anniversary of the Saviour's birth.

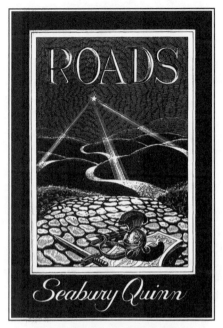

Made in United States
Troutdale, OR
01/05/2025

27626110R00076